DOWN ON THE FARM WITH

GROVER

by Ray Sipherd

Illustrated by
Eleanor Mill

*Featuring Jim Henson's
Sesame Street Muppets*

A SESAME STREET/GOLDEN PRESS BOOK
Published by Western Publishing Company, Inc.
in conjunction with Children's Television Workshop.

One spring day everybody was
surprised to see Grover coming down
Sesame Street wearing overalls and
a big straw hat.

"Hello, everybodee!" called
Grover. "Guess what I am going
to be. A farmer!

"My uncle wants me to take care of his farm this weekend while he is away."

"Do you know how to be a farmer, Grover?" asked Bert.

"Oh, I am sure that being a farmer is easy," he answered. "I, lovable, furry old Grover, can do it."

And he waved good-bye.

When Grover arrived at his uncle's farm, he saw a farmhouse and a big barn with animals in the barnyard. He saw the fruit trees. His uncle also showed him the fields where vegetables grew every year.

"There are so many things a farmer has to do!" Grover's uncle told him. "I'll show you what they are."

First Grover's uncle showed him how to give feed to the chickens and ducks and hay to the cows and horses.

Then Grover's uncle showed him how to milk a cow.

"Taking care of animals is only part of a farmer's job," Grover's uncle told him. "There is also farm machinery to run, like this tractor and plow.

"After you've plowed the furrows in the field, you can plant the seeds that will grow into vegetables, such as corn and potatoes and string beans."

Finally, after Grover's uncle had shown Grover all the chores to do on the farm, he drove away.

"Now I am Grover the Farmer!" thought Grover as he waved good-bye to his uncle.

The next morning it was time to feed the animals again.

"Wait a minute!" said Grover. "I bet these cute little animals are tired of all that old hay and oats. I will fix them something special and delicious!"

So Grover cooked his own favorite foods for the animals to eat.

Grover took the food to the barn.

"Hello, everybodee! Here is your breakfast!" he
called to the animals. "I made you some of my favorite
things—hamburgers and pizza and milk shakes and
spaghetti and ice cream!"

Grover was surprised that none of the animals
wanted the food he had cooked.

Then Grover tried to milk the cow.
"Oh, my goodness," he said. "I wonder
why there is no milk coming out."

Next he tried to clean the pig pen.
"Oh, this is very messy," said Grover.
"Oops!" He tripped over his bucket and fell
headfirst into the mud. "Being a farmer
is harder than I thought!"

However, Grover the Farmer was not discouraged.
He climbed up on the tractor and began to plow the field.
But he couldn't remember how to stop.
"AIEEEE!" cried Grover, as he crashed into the
chicken coop.

Finally Grover began to plant.
"These tiny seeds will grow up into squash and corn and beans and peas and tomatoes," he said. "Isn't that wonderful?"

"Hello, birdees!"
Grover called to a flock
of birds flying above
him.

The birds flew
down onto the field and
began eating the seeds
that Grover had planted.

So Grover had to plant seeds all over again.
"At last!" thought Grover. "The crops are planted
and nothing else can go wrong!"

All at once it began to rain.
It rained ... and *rained* ... and *RAINED!*
When the rain stopped, the wind began to blow.
It blew ... and *blew* ... and *BLEW!*

Grover looked at what the rain and wind had done
to the farm.

"Being a farmer is *much* harder than I thought!"
he said.

As the sky cleared, Grover looked up and saw all
his friends from Sesame Street hurrying toward him.
"Oh, no!" said Grover. "Here comes everybody!
What will my friends say when they see this mess? Oh,
I am so embarrassed!"

But Grover's friends pitched right in to help him. And by the time Grover's uncle came home to the farm, everything was all fixed and the chores were almost done.

And when fall came, the Sesame Street gang returned to help with the harvest. They picked the fruits from the trees and the vegetables from the field. Then they loaded the fruit and vegetables onto the farm wagon to be taken into town to be sold.

"I am a good farmer after all," said Grover. "Oh, I am so proud!"

ABCDEFGH